This igloo book belongs to:

....

MY MONSTER SMELLS GROSS!

Written by
Nicky Lander

SCRATCH AND SNIFF BOOK

igloobooks

One day I found a monster,
hiding inside the laundry box.
He was curled up asleep,
in a pile of my smelly socks.

He had spiky, red hair,
big horns and furry skin.
And when he woke up he smiled at me
with a big, toothy grin.

I asked him what his name was,
but he just laughed and said with glee,
"I'm the grossest monster you'll ever meet,
come and play with me!"

We spent the day together,
getting muddy, stinky and smelly.
Me and my monster even made
home-made pink worm jelly!

My monster likes revolting stuff,
like furry moths and slugs.
He also loves to suck the goo
from different sorts of bugs!

But the grimy, gross, disgusting
dish my monster likes the most,
is sickeningly squiggly, wriggly maggots
spread on mouldy toast!

My monster likes to look his best,
everywhere he goes.
He bathes in slimy swamps and trims
the green claws on his toes.

He smoothes his hair with fish oil and
cleans his teeth with mouldy goo.
Under his arms he rubs old cheese
and that smells stinky, too!

In my tree house my monster plays
all sorts of naughty tricks.
He picks big lumps of ear wax,
then licks his lips and flicks!

He loves to make big, sloppy cakes
and horrid cupcakes, too.
He covers them in mud and mould
and sometimes soft bird poo!

At my birthday party,
he put a yucky outfit on.
His waistcoat was made with snail shells
stuck together with chewing gum.

His shorts were covered with stringy slime
and crusty old cowpats.
On his hat were pink mouse tails
and flapping vampire bats!

Sometimes he gets greasy spots.
They're squishy and they're green.
When he's got a big one,
you'll know where he's been.

He loves to squeeze and squash it
and squish it, 'til it spurts.
He just loves to see how far
he can make the green pus squirt!

My monster loves a game of pretend,
we play it all the time.
We imagine we are pirates,
sailing on a sea of slime.

Our ship's flag is made from his old pants
and we wear grubby pirate vests.
We fight scary sea monsters
and use maps to find treasure chests.

My monster has got awful wind,
from eating lots of beans.
He can eat ten cans at once,
and you know what that means?

He puts on his helmet
and into his cart he hops.
He counts from one to ten,
then lets out windy pops!

My monster once rode in a hot air balloon,
up and up it soared.
But it wasn't long before my monster
got very, very bored.

He picked a fresh bogey,
loaded his catapult and pulled it back.
The bogies flew through the sky
and hit the poor birds with a thwack!

When we go away on holiday,
my monster never behaves.
Last year he got me lost
in some slimy, grimy caves.

He stomped in lots of sandcastles
and I always got the blame.
But a holiday without him
just wouldn't be the same.

I know that my monster is naughty
and never does what he's told,
and that he loves to eat smelly
mud and bird poo and mould.

But even though he's imaginary and
really just pretend,
He'll always be my super smelly,
very best friend.